TO BABI BANG

First published 2011 by Walker Books Ltd, 87 Vauxhall Walk, London SE11 5HJ

2 4 6 8 10 9 7 5 3 1

© 2011 Petr Horáček

The right of Petr Horáček to be identified as author/illustrator of this work has been asserted
by him in accordance with the Copyright, Designs and Patents Act 1988

This book has been typeset in Futura T Light

Printed in China

British Library Cataloguing in Publication Data:
a catalogue record for this book is available from the British Library

Hardback: ISBN 978-1-4063-2460-0
Paperback: ISBN 978-1-4063-3402-9

www.walker.co.uk

Puffin PETER

Petr Horáček

WALKER BOOKS
AND SUBSIDIARIES
LONDON • BOSTON • SYDNEY • AUCKLAND

This is **PETER**.

This is **PAUL**.

Peter and Paul
were the best of friends.

Paul made Peter laugh by being
funny and noisy. They spent their
days happily fishing around
their rocky island.

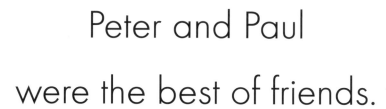

One day,
while they were
out diving ...

a storm
blew up.

A big,

big storm.

Peter was lost.

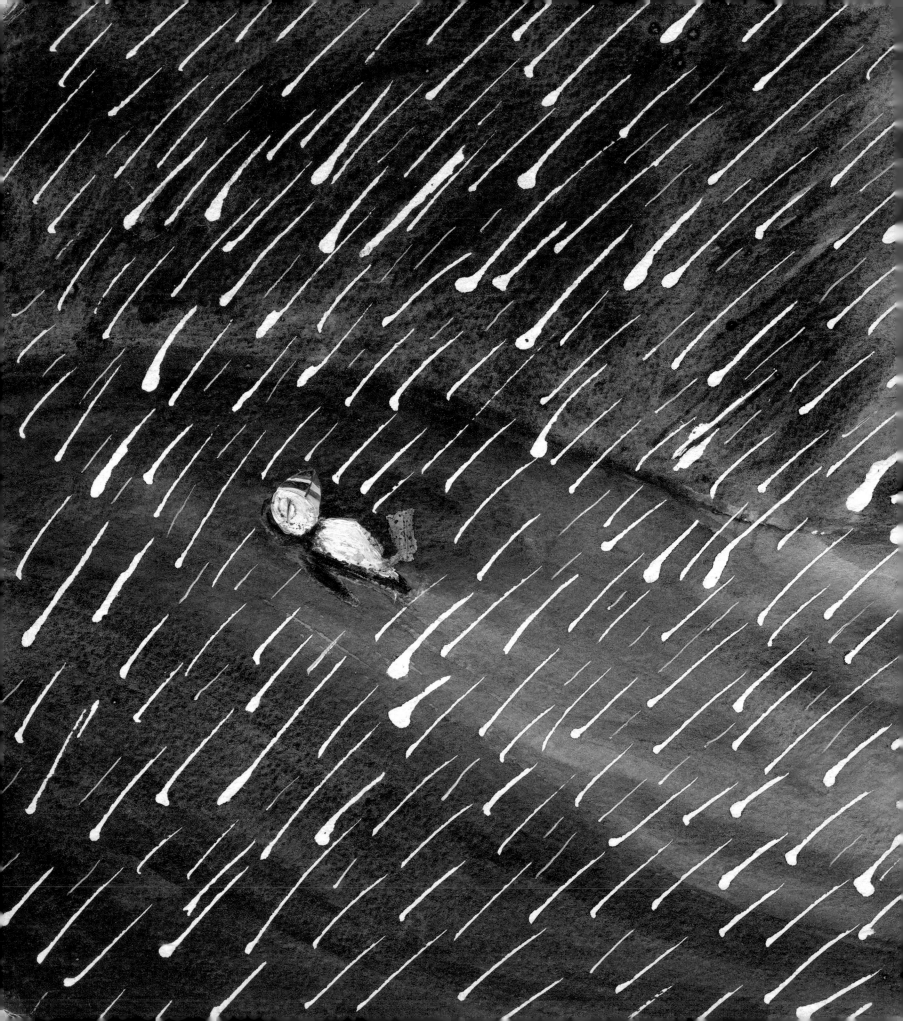

He was

blown far out

to sea.

At last the storm was over.

"Where am I?" said Peter.

He opened his eyes.

"And where is Paul?"

"Hello,"
said the kind whale.
"Are you lost?"

"Yes," said Peter.

"And I've lost my best friend Paul."

"What's he like?" said the whale.

"Oh! Paul is funny and noisy.

Can you help me find him?"

"Funny and noisy. I know just where to look," said the whale, and they set off together.

"Here we are," said the whale
as they arrived on a small island.

"Which one is Paul?"

The birds were funny and noisy,
but they were *nothing* like Paul.

"Paul is not a parrot,"
said Peter. "Paul's feathers
are black and white!"

"Funny, noisy and black and white?" said the whale. "I know just where to look." And off they set. "Here we are. It's rather cold."

The birds were funny, noisy and black and white, but they were *nothing* like Paul.

"Paul is not a penguin," said Peter.

"Paul's beak is very colourful."

"Funny, noisy, black and white, with a colourful beak," said the whale. "I know exactly where to look." And they set off again. The bird on the island was funny, noisy, black and white with a colourful beak, but he wasn't Paul.

"Paul is not a toucan," said Peter.

"We are never going to find him."

Peter was very sad.

The whale didn't know where
else to look, so they drifted
across the ocean.

After a few days some tiny islands

appeared on the horizon.

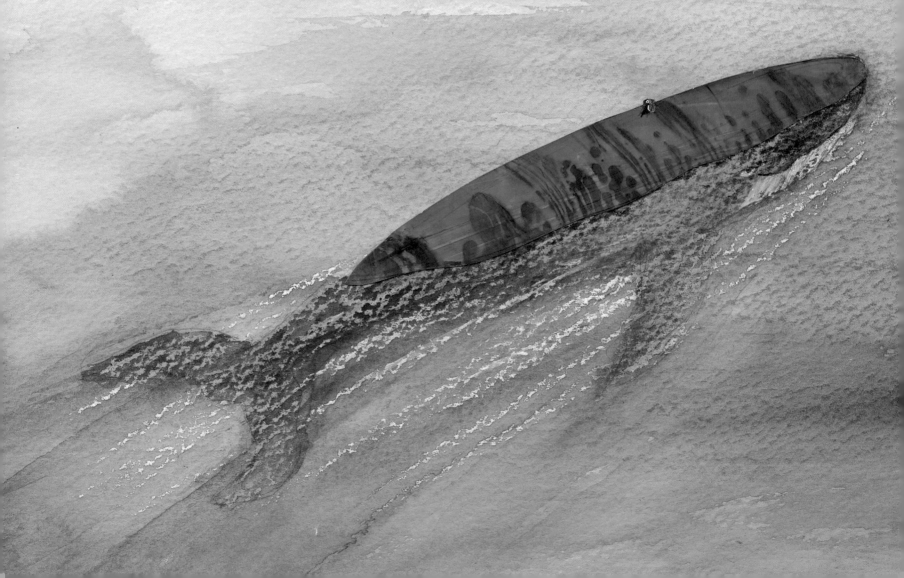

Peter was too sad to look as he drifted towards them.

"Look!" said the whale. "What's that?"

It was

black and white,

with a

colourful beak.

It was
funny and noisy...

It
was
PAUL!

Peter was overjoyed.

"So this is Paul," cried the whale.

"Why didn't you tell me?"

"Tell you what?" said Peter.

The whale smiled.

"That he's a puffin, just like you!"

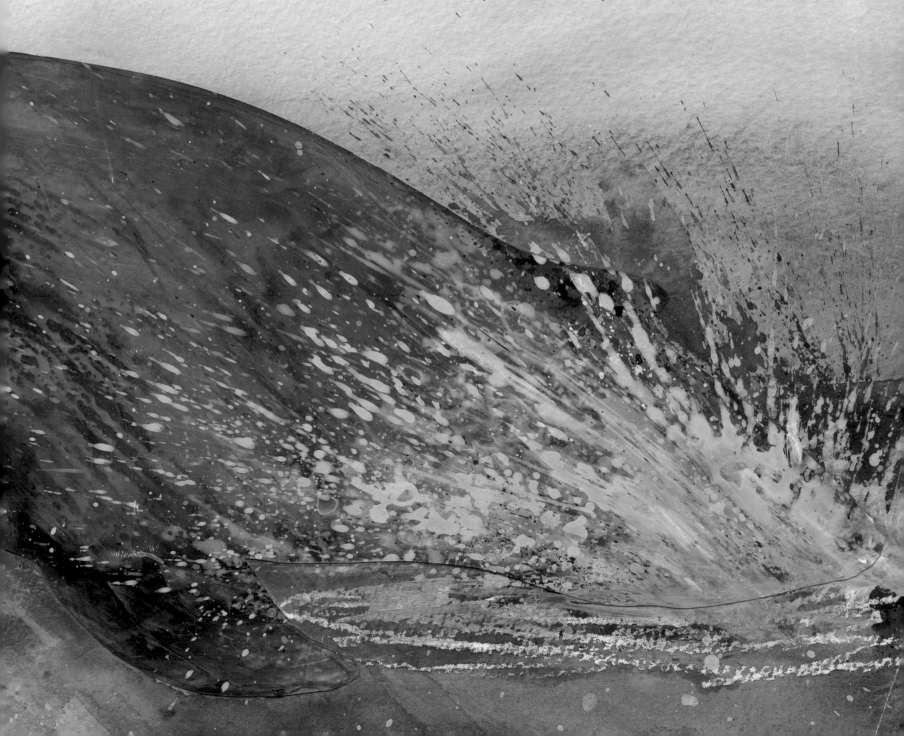